ABOUT THIS BOOK: The illustrations for this book were done in watercolor, acrylic ink, oil pastel, and colored pencil. This book was edited by Deirdre Jones and designed by Nicole Brown with art direction by Jen Keenan. The production was supervised by Virginia Lawther, and the production editor was Marisa Finkelstein. The text was set in Berliner Grotesk.

THREE GRUMPY TRUCKS

WRITTEN BY **TODD TARPLEY**

ILLUSTRATED BY **GUY PARKER-REES**

LB

Little, Brown and Company
New York Boston

Across the sandbox, down the slide.
Through the sprinkler, side by side.

Three little trucks were scooping, shifting, grating, grinding, loading, lifting.

Hours later, bright sun beating.
Three tired engines overheating.
Fuel gauges running low.

"Little trucks, it's time to—"

"Five more minutes! Let us stay!"
"Okay? Okay? **Okay?**"

Hoses hissing, warnings beeping.
Red lights flashing, fluids seeping.
Fuses now about to blow.

"Please, little trucks, it's time to go!
Your temp's too high! Your fuel's too low!
Your windshield fluids are smelling strange!
I think you need a wiper change!"

"Okay, okay,
OKAY! We KNOW!
ONE MORE MINUTE—
THEN WE'LL GO!"

Engines smoking, motors failing.
Tailpipes clanging, rotors flailing.

They made an awful screeching sound.
They banged their bumpers on the ground.

They stomped, they whomped,
they sparked, they spit.
They honked, they bonked,
they threw a fit.

What could she do?
What could she say?

To calm them down?
To save the day?

She soothed the little trucks' alarms,
then gathered them into her arms.
Their undersides were caked in oil.
Their bumpers dark with soot and soil.

She towed them home still in a daze...

...then set them in their engine bays.
Their spark plugs charged, their tires exchanged,

their windshields washed, their wipers changed,
their bumpers polished up—and THEN...